Gavin and Errol and Sophie

and Sushma and David and Kate

and Robert and Alison are . . .

...Starting School

Janet and Allan Ahlberg

PUFFIN BOOKS

For
Val Dwelly, who gave us the idea
and
Birstall Riverside Primary School, who let us in.

The First Day

The children wait
in the playground

with their mums and
dads and brothers and

sisters ... and a puppy.

The bell rings.

Gavin and Errol

and Sophie and

Sushma  and David

and Kate and Robert and Alison

go into the school

and meet their teacher.

They hang
their hats and
coats in the cloakroom, have a look

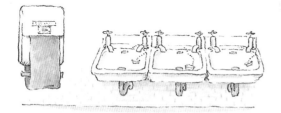 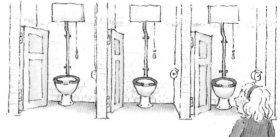

at the toilets and go
into the classroom. They sit on the mat
with the rest of the class.

The teacher calls the register and collects the dinner money.

She shows the children round the classroom,  and the parents too.

In the classroom there are  tables chairs and drawers for the children to keep their things in.  There is ...

a book corner

a home corner

an interest table

a box of dressing up clothes

and a baby rabbit

in a rabbit hutch.

During the morning  Gavin

and Errol  and Sophie

and Sushma and David

and Kate

and Robert and

Alison get used to the classroom

 and the rabbit gets used

to them.

At play time...

they go out to play.

At dinner time they eat their dinners.

In the afternoon they draw pictures,

go out to play again and have

singing in the hall.

At the end of the day they

tidy up,

have a story on the mat,

put on their hats and coats —

and go home.

The Second Day

The next day Gavin and Errol and

Sophie and Sushma and David and

Kate and Robert and Alison

go to school again.

  In the morning
they do a picture
and some writing in their new books.

 After that they
have music and
movement in the hall.

Errol's mum
plays the
piano.

At play time Robert loses his hat ... and Alison finds it.

Errol bangs his knee,

and the teacher rubs it better.

Gavin and Sushma and David climb on the climbing frame.

Kate <u>thinks</u> about climbing.

In the afternoon the children make

some models.

They show them to the

head teacher, have a story

on the mat and go home.

The First Week

As the days go by,

the children

get more used to the school.

On Wednesday they go into the hall for assembly.

They listen to the singing and say a prayer.

They watch some older children do a play.

On Thursday they start learning to read.

Run, run as fast as you can.

Stop, stop little boy. Said the horse

He jumped onto the fox's back.

Gavin can read already.

He brings his book from  home to show the teacher.

Errol brings his <u>tooth</u>

to show the teacher.

It came out in the night.

On Friday they go swimming in the school pool.

The water is warm and not deep. Robert

and Sushma and Kate jump up and down.

David and Sophie walk in down the steps.

Errol <u>thinks</u> about walking in.

In the afternoon Kate and Sushma and

David do cooking

with David's mum.

They make 12 little cakes,

3 big cakes

...and a mess.

Time Goes By

The next week Gavin  and

Errol and Sophie

and Sushma

and David

and Kate

and

Robert and Alison...

choose a name for the rabbit.

They draw rabbit  pictures,

make rabbit models,

bake rabbit biscuits,

have rabbit stories on the mat, and do

lots more rabbit

things besides.

The week after that the children
have their photographs taken.

And the week after that
Gavin loses a glove,

and Alison learns to swim;

Sophie reads  a book,

and Sushma shows her sari

and her Diva  lamp.

Robert <u>thinks</u> about being in a

hallowe'en play.

And sometimes the children

are happy,

and sometimes they are sad;

sometimes puzzled – or sleepy –

or grumpy – or lumpy – or spotty!

Sometimes
the teacher is not
cheerful either.

End of Term

Christmas comes.

In the last week of term the infants

do a play about

baby Jesus.

Everybody has a part,

and all the mums

and dads come

to watch.

On the last <u>day</u> of term
the children bring cakes

and crisps,

sausages, sandwiches

and jellies, and have a party

Merry Christmas Ronald

in the classroom.

Then Gavin and Errol
and Sophie

and Sushma

and Kate

and David

and Robert and Alison

go home...

and the holiday begins.